www.mcsweeneys.net

Manufactured in China by Shanghai Offset

ISBN: 978-1-938073-78-6

First edition

LEMONY SNICKET
29 MYTHS ON THE SWINSTER PHARMACY

illustrations by Lisa Brown

We are very curious about the Swinster Pharmacy.
We travelled all the way from the next town
to find out what it sells.

2.

Inside the window are three Styrofoam heads wearing wigs.
Inside, the employees wear coats in the same shade of white.
We followed one of them home one night
and he lived in a house right across from another pharmacy.

The employee, not the coat.

3. Rumors around town say there are four secrets
about the Swinster Pharmacy,
but no one knows what any of them are.

4. By the counter there are pieces of fruit in a bowl.
There are some large fruits like apples and bananas,
and some grapes. They are all cut in half.
You can take a piece if you want to,
but I never do.

The grapes aren't cut in half.

5.

One time the news did a story about all the arson in town, and they panned the street with the Swinster Pharmacy on it.

This is usually a quiet town,

they said, and the camera panned the street with the Swinster Pharmacy on it.

6. My friend said that when people
are walking down the street casually,
just snacking or whispering or something,
they usually stop
when they pass the Swinster Pharmacy.

7. They used to keep a book rack out front,
but one day it disappeared.
As if anyone would want to buy
a romance or a mystery or another book
at the Swinster Pharmacy.

8.

We like to sneak up on the Swinster Pharmacy.
We stay on the other side of the street as long as possible,
lurking behind trees in quiet yellow light, or sometimes in the evening.

9. I was going to write a poem about the Swinster Pharmacy.

10. A woman went in once and came out fifteen minutes later wearing the exact same outfit.

What do they sell there?

11.

When the town aches,
the Swinster Pharmacy aches with it.

12.

In all of our dreams
the Pharmacy squats in the middle of the block
like something blue and hungry.
In the morning it is on the corner.

13. I think the Swinster Pharmacy is closed on weekends.

Your lies bounce off its windows like spinning discarded tops.

15. The building is a perfect square.
We measured it last night.

16.

The owner of the Swinster Pharmacy is completely insane and quite tall.
He arrives before we wake up but everyone sees him leave.
I *think* he's the owner.

Something about the door is electric,
electric as opposed to acoustic.
It closes with a hiss,
like the serpent in the Garden of Eden
or a slow, dead tire.

19.

Late one night,
strange music came out of the Swinster Pharmacy,
but it turned out to be a radio.

20.

Three pets have gone missing within a block of the Swinster Pharmacy in the last fourteen years.

21.

An out-of-town policeman
said you could buy aspirin
and toothpaste there,
just like anyone else.

22.

Nothing's perfect.
The Swinster Pharmacy is not perfect.
The glow of the moon on the car, there,
is not perfect.

23.

Kiss me,

she thought somebody whispered
from the corner,
but it was too late to stop running.

25.

The fire department got a phone call.
The voice said it was the Swinster Pharmacy,
but it turned out to be another pharmacy
that burned to the ground before anyone arrived.
The smoke took hours to clear.

26.

What time is it? It's late.

I'm not allowed to talk about the Swinster Pharmacy.

27. Dogs bark at it all the time.

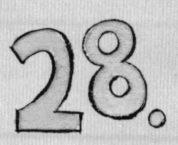

28.

"What do they sell there?
Just tell us that, please,
what do they sell there?"
That's what the newspaper asked.
But he wouldn't tell them.

29.

People get sick all the time,
but nobody gets better
because of the Swinster Pharmacy.